08/2011

PALM BEACH COUNTY
LIBRARY SYSTEM
3650 Summit Boulevard
West Palm Beach, FL 33406-4198

DAV PILKEY

ORCHARD BOOKS / NEW YORK
An Imprint of Scholastic Inc.

THE DRAGON TALES

Copyright © 1991 by Dav Pilkey
All rights reserved. Published by Orchard Books,
an imprint of Scholastic Inc., *Publishers since 1920.*
ORCHARD BOOKS and design are registered trademarks of Watts
Publishing Group, Ltd., used under license. SCHOLASTIC and associated
logos are trademarks and/or registered trademarks of Scholastic Inc..
No part of this publication may be reproduced, stored in a
retrieval system, or transmitted in any form or by any means,
electronic, mechanical, photocopying, recording, or
otherwise, without written permission of the publisher.
For information regarding permission, write to
Orchard Books, Scholastic Inc., Permissions Department,
557 Broadway, New York, NY 10012.
Library of Congress Cataloging-in-Publication Data
Pilkey, Dav, / date. A Friend for Dragon.
Dragon's first tale / Dav Pilkey. p. cm (The Dragon tales)
Summary: Dragon becomes such close friends
with an apple that he deeply mourns its loss and
is overjoyed when more grow to take its place.
ISBN-10: 0-531-07054-9 / ISBN-13: 978-0-531-07054-3 (pbk.)
[I. Dragons—Fiction. 2. Apple—Fiction. 3. Friendship—
Fiction.] I. Title. II. Series. Dragon tales.
PZ7.P63123Fr 1991 [E]—dc20 90045219
51 50 49 11 12 13/0
Printed in the U.S.A. 40
The illustrations are watercolor with pencil,
reproduced in full-color.
This Orchard Books edition, September 2007

Contents

For Cyndi

1

A Friend for Dragon

There once was a blue dragon
who lived in a little house
all by himself.
Sometimes Dragon got lonely.

“I wish I had a friend,” said Dragon.
So he went out into the world
to look for a friend.

Dragon went to the woods
and met a small black squirrel.

"Will you be my friend?"
said Dragon.

"No," said the squirrel.
"I'm too busy."

Dragon went to the riverbank
and met a fat gray hippo.

"Will you be my friend?"
said Dragon.

"No," said the hippo,
"I'm too tired."

Dragon went to the pond
and met a slick green crocodile.

"Will you be my friend?"
said Dragon.

"No," said the crocodile.
"I'm too grouchy."

So Dragon sat down under a tree,
still wishing for a friend.
Suddenly, an apple fell
out of the tree and hit Dragon
on the head.

Just then, a little green snake
slithered by. The snake wanted
to play a joke on Dragon.
So it hid behind a rock
and called out, "Hi, Dragon."

Dragon looked all around,
but he didn't see anyone.
"Who said that?" cried Dragon.

"I did," said the snake.
Dragon looked all around again,
but he still didn't see anyone.

“Where are you?” said Dragon.

“I’m right here in your hand,” said the snake.

Dragon looked at the apple in his hand
and scratched his big head.

“I did not know apples could talk,”
said Dragon.

“Oh, but we can,”
said the snake in the grass.

"Would you like to be my friend?"
Dragon asked the apple.

"Oh, yes," laughed the snake.

"At last," said Dragon.
"A friend."

2
Friends at Home

Dragon took the apple home
and built a warm, cozy fire.
He told spooky stories to the apple.
He told funny jokes to the apple.
Dragon talked all day long
and into the night.

"You are a good listener,"
said Dragon. "Good friends
are always good listeners."

Dragon fixed a midnight snack.
He mixed cookies, orange juice,
and catsup all together in a big bowl.
Dragon scooped some of the food
onto his plate. Then he scooped
some food onto the apple's plate.

"Just say 'When,'" said Dragon.
The apple did not say "When."
So Dragon scooped some more food
onto the apple's plate.

"Just say 'When,'" Dragon said.
The apple still did not say "When."

So Dragon scooped the rest of the food onto the apple's plate.

"I am glad that we both like to eat so much," said Dragon. "Good friends should always have a lot in common."

Dragon ate up all of his food.
The apple did not eat any food at all.
Dragon was still hungry.
He looked at the apple's plate
and drooled.

"Do you mind if I eat some
of your food?" asked Dragon.
The apple did not seem to mind.

So Dragon ate up all of the apple's food too.

"You are a good friend," said Dragon. "Good friends always share."

3
The New Day

The next morning, Dragon awoke
with the sun.

"Good morning, Apple," said Dragon.
The apple did not answer.
So Dragon went out to the kitchen
and made breakfast.

When he was finished eating,
he tried to wake the apple up again.
"Good morning, Apple," he cried.
The apple still did not answer.

So Dragon went outside for a walk
along the riverbank.
When he came back, he tried to wake
the apple up again.
"GOOD MORNING, APPLE!" he screamed.
The apple still did not answer.

Dragon was very worried.
He called the doctor.
"My apple won't talk to me,"
said Dragon.

"Maybe it's a crab apple,"
said the doctor.

"No," said Dragon. "I think
it is sick."

So Dragon took the apple
to the doctor's office.
They sat down next to a big walrus.

"What's the matter with you?"
asked the walrus.

"It's my apple," said Dragon.
"It won't talk to me."

The walrus stared at the apple
and drooled.

Dragon needed a drink of water.
"Will you watch my apple for me?"
Dragon asked the walrus.

"Sure," said the walrus,
licking her lips.

When Dragon came back, the apple had changed.
It was not round anymore.
It was not shiny anymore.
It was not red anymore.
Now it was wet and skinny and white.

"What happened to you?" cried Dragon.
"Are you all right?"

The little white thing did not answer.

Dragon wrapped his friend
in a piece of paper
and carried it home.
"Don't worry," said Dragon.
"Everything will be OK."

When Dragon got home,
the little white thing had turned all
mushy and brown.

“Are you hurt?” asked Dragon.
The mushy brown thing did not answer.
“Are you sick?” asked Dragon.
But there was no answer.
“Are you dead?” asked Dragon.
Still, there was no answer.

Dragon scratched his big head
and started to cry.

4
Good-bye

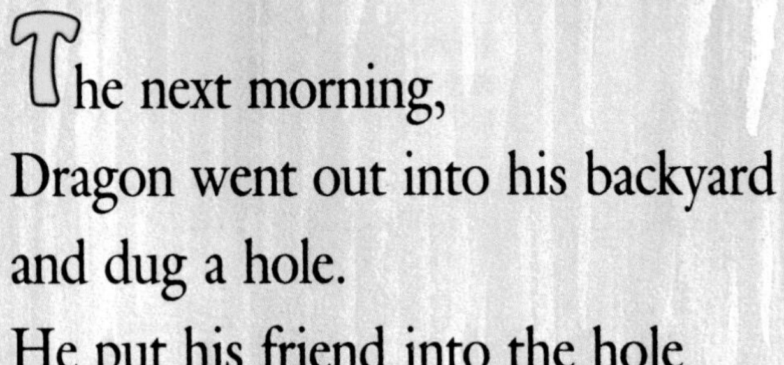

The next morning,
Dragon went out into his backyard
and dug a hole.
He put his friend into the hole
and covered it over with dirt.

Dragon made a sign.
On the sign, he wrote the word
"Friend."

Dragon was very sad.
He cried every day.
He did not want to eat.
He could not get to sleep.
Dragon did not leave his house
for a long, long time.

But after a while,
Dragon stopped being so sad.
He cried less and less.
He began to eat and sleep better.

Still, he was very lonely.

5
Summertime

One day, many months later,
Dragon walked out into his backyard.
He was still feeling lonely.
Dragon sat down under the big tree
growing in his yard.
He wished for a friend.
Suddenly, something fell
out of the tree and hit Dragon
on the head.

It was an apple.

Then Dragon looked up, and smiled.